D0570948

Splitting Up

Kate Petty, Lisa Kopper, and Jim Pipe

Stargazer Books
Mankato, Minnesota

© Aladdin Books Ltd 2009
Designed and produced by
Aladdin Books Ltd

First published in 2009
in the United States by
Stargazer Books,
distributed by Black Rabbit Books
PO Box 3263, Mankato, MN 56002

Illustrator: Lisa Kopper   Photocredits: All photos from istockphoto.com.

Library of Congress Cataloging-in-Publication Data

Petty, Kate.
  Splitting up / Kate Petty.
     p. cm. -- (My first time)
  Summary: Little Maria learns to deal with her parents' separation.
  Includes index.
  ISBN 978-1-59604-174-5
  [1. Parent and child--Fiction. 2. Separation (Psychology)--Fiction.] I. Title.
  PZ7.P44814Sp 2009
  [E]--dc22
                          2008015281

About this book

New experiences can be scary for young children. This series will help them to understand situations they may find themselves in, by explaining in a friendly way what can happen.

This book can be used as a starting point for discussing issues. The questions in some of the boxes ask children about their own experiences.

The stories will also help children to master basic reading skills and learn new vocabulary.

It can help if you read the first sentence to children, and then encourage them to read the rest of the page or story. At the end, try looking through the book again to find where the words in the glossary are used.

Contents

Sam wishes Maria hadn't come to play.
She doesn't want to build a camp.

She doesn't want to make mud pies.
She doesn't want to make cakes.

4

Maria is curled up in a chair watching TV.

"Would you like a cake, Maria?"
"No." Maria isn't hungry.

What do you do when you feel sad?

5

Sam is quite glad when Maria's mom
comes to take her home.

Maria runs into her mom's
arms and hugs her tightly.

Maria's mom doesn't look very happy either.

"I'm not getting along very well with
Maria's dad at the moment," she says.
"We're all feeling a bit unsettled."

At school, Sam feels fed up with Maria.
She argues about everything.

She threw a plate at him in the
home corner. It made Sam cry.

"I don't like you any more, Maria," says Sam.
"Nobody does," says Maria to the teacher.

"Mom and Dad just argue all the time.
They won't stop even when I ask them to."

Do you argue
with anyone?

Sam talks to Mom about his day.
"You and Dad argue, don't you?"

Mom says everybody argues
now and then. "Dad and I make up
because we're good friends."

10

"Sometimes parents stop being friends and they can't make up after arguments.

Then it might be easier for everybody if they didn't live together anymore."

Today Sam is playing at Maria's house.
"Where's your dad, Maria?"

Maria doesn't want to tell Sam.
Her mom says he's gone away for a while.

12

"I miss my dad," says Maria,
"but Mom isn't as sad as she used to be."

"Dad also takes me out alot.
You can come with us one day."

When Sam gets home
he plays with Dad.
"Will you ever leave us, Dad?"

"I don't want to leave, Sam.
I'd be lonely without all of you."

Do you ever
feel lonely?

"Do you think Maria's dad is lonely?"

"I expect he misses Maria as much as she misses him. It's hard for them all but it's better that they stop fighting."

15

Goal! Sam is playing soccer with Maria and her dad.

"Can we go to the adventure playground now?"
This is fun!

16

What do you like doing with your mom or dad?

Maria's dad buys
them fries and
milkshakes for lunch.

There's time for
one more ride
on the spaceship
before they go home.

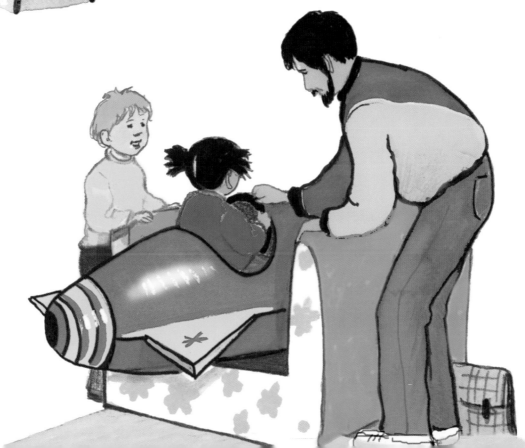

17

A few weeks later Maria has some news.
Her dad has moved into a new apartment.

There's a bedroom specially for her
and she can keep some things there.

Maria shows Sam around the apartment.
There isn't much in it yet!

Sam thinks it might be nice
to have two homes to go to.

Maria likes both her homes.

She wishes her mom and dad could be happy again but she's glad they're both happier than they used to be.

Maria still feels a bit sad when her dad says goodbye.

But he has promised that wherever he lives he will always love her.

"Goodbye Dad!" "Hello Mom!"

How do you say goodbye?

hugging

arguing

talking

playing

lunch

having
two homes

Index

Find out more

Find out more about when parents split up:

www.kidsturn.org
www.kidshealth.org
www.divorcecare.com
www.dealwithdivorce.com

24